The Running Girls
a novelette

BRIA BURTON

Soul Attitude Press

The Running Girls
Copyright © 2017 by Bria Burton

The Running Girls appears in ebook format previously copyrighted in 2016.

This a work of fiction. Names, characters, places and incidents are either the product of the author's imagination, or, if real, used fictitiously.

Published by Soul Attitude Press
PO Box 1656
Pinellas Park, FL 33782
www.soulattitudepress.com
soulattitudepress@gmail.com
Cover Artist: Bria Burton
Shoe glyph created with Pixabay.com by Bria Burton
www.briaburton.com

ISBN 978-1-946338-14-3

First Edition

ACKNOWLEDGMENTS

"I'll never run a marathon." Those words once escaped my lips. Yet here I am, four marathons later. Not to mention the dozens of half marathons, 15Ks, 10Ks, and 5Ks. To top it off, I work at a fantastic running store.

I must thank the owners of St. Pete Running Company, Janna and Cody Angell. They have given me more expertise, advice, and opportunity than they will probably ever know.

When it comes to running and writing, many people inspire me. Thank you, dear family and friends, for all the ways you have helped shape me into the person I am today. I have a few special thank you messages to share.

To my sister in Christ, Terry. Thank you for your time, your fellowship, your encouragement, and for being you! This story wouldn't have happened without your suggestion that I write it.

To Alyssa, my heart and soul. You inspired the premise of this story because you've done five hundred miles in one summer, among other earth-shattering feats. You are a source of constant amazement for me.

Endless thank yous to all my writing friends: Brenda, Cate, and Maria get extra gratitude for their overtime critiquing skills. Many thanks to Rachel, Seth, Martin, Cheri, Alice, and Sue. A special thank you to John Rehg of Soul Attitude Press who helped make this print book possible.

Mom and Dad, there were times in my youth when you made me do things I didn't want to do. Thank you for that. I learned so much from those experiences, and this story is a direct result.

To my husband. Thank you for always supporting and loving me. And to our soon-to-be-born baby boy, I can't wait to meet you!

To my Lord. You gave me a love for storytelling, and I thank you for the inspiration and the gift of writing.

For all girls who run, and especially for those who have been close to my heart.

Table of Contents

1. 500-Mile Summer of '89

"*How* many miles?" Clara's mom stopped stirring the ramen noodles. She paused in front of the stove with the wooden spoon hovering over the simmering pot. Her widening eyes gave Clara a knot in her stomach. This conversation wasn't going to be as simple as she'd hoped.

"Coach McFarland gave the whole team a speech about what it means to be a serious runner. Well, that's what I want to be," Clara said, straightening her posture as she admitted the truth out loud.

Freshman through junior year in high school, she'd been a sub-par member of the cross country team. Only one other person was slower than Clara, and she'd just graduated. Yesterday, Coach McFarland had invited the whole team to his house for a barbecue potluck where he'd given a speech that touched Clara's heart in a way she hadn't expected.

Clara's parents had only been able to pick her up afterward, not take her, so she'd gotten a ride with Missy Underwood, the fastest girl on the team. Even though they were both going to be seniors, Clara didn't really know how to talk to Missy. They'd been in most of the same classes since fifth grade, but Missy was popular. It had taken Clara all day to muster up the courage to ask for the ride to Coach's barbecue.

"Um. Sure," Missy had replied. "But you'll have to sit in back because Paula is riding with me, too."

Clara had felt so grateful that she didn't mind the stipulation. Missy's brand new 1989 Toyota Camry gleamed. Clara had brushed her fingers back and forth along the leather seat the whole ride. Her parents wouldn't buy her a car, so she was stuck taking the bus and mooching rides until she could afford one. On the way, with a Madonna cassette playing in the background, Missy and Paula gossiped about everything. They bashed teachers, fellow students (even the ones Clara thought they were friends with), and their parents.

"What are your parents like, Clara?" Paula had asked as the car pulled to a stop in front of Coach's house, giving her hardly any time to respond.

"They're pretty cool. I guess," she said as the pair of them popped out of the car. They walked ahead of Clara and didn't acknowledge her the rest of the evening.

Clara wished she'd had the opportunity to spill her feelings about her mom. Maybe not to Missy and Paula, but to someone who would listen and care. Clara didn't want to be a ball of anxiety like her mom could be. For once she wanted to take a risk without being told everything that could go wrong.

"Honey, do you realize what you're saying?" Her mom stirred the noodles and spoke slowly, talking to Clara as if she were eight years old. "500 miles is way more than you've ever done, let alone in one summer."

"That's because I never cared if I was any good. Now I do." Mediocrity reigned in Clara's life. She was an average student, a below-average athlete, and no one, including her parents, made her feel like she should strive for anything. She only had two close friends. Beth and Ashleigh were a year ahead of her. She felt left behind even before the graduation ceremony. Beth had been valedictorian while Ashleigh was salutatorian. With high school officially over for them, everything was about prepping for freshman year of college. They kept busy with summer jobs. Clara saw the writing on the wall. They would forget her, if they hadn't already.

As a seventeen-year-old about to enter senior year, Clara didn't have much to show for her life. When Coach had interrupted the small talk at the barbecue to address everyone, he didn't say much. But what he'd said sent chills through Clara.

"I challenge each and every cross country team member to complete the 500-mile summer challenge," Coach had said, his hand on his wife's shoulder. They were the picture of opposites attract: he was a towering black man who commanded the attention of a room without the need for a microphone, and she was a tiny, light-skinned woman who barely spoke.

Every year at the beginning of cross country season, Coach told the story of how they had met twenty years ago while he was stationed in Heidelberg, Germany. His military buzz cut had intimidated Clara until she realized that Coach McFarland was more of a teddy bear than a drill sergeant.

"I won't bang on your door to make sure you get up in the morning and do your miles. That's on you," he had said. "If you want to be a serious runner, here is your chance. Remember this: today is the first day of the rest of your lives."

Clara's arm hairs had stood on end. She didn't want to be average any more.

That morning, she'd gotten up and done a five-mile jog. Slowly, but she'd done it and felt pretty good. After showering, she'd found an unused journal in a drawer and wrote down what Coach had said. *Today is the first day of the rest of my life.*

Again the words had impacted her like a smack to her chest. Her heart pounded, and bumps raised on her arms and legs. Below the quote she had written,

500-Mile Summer Challenge
Day 1: 5 miles complete
Total miles: 5

"I'm doing this, Mom." Clara ignored the look of trepidation etched like a mask on her mother's face.

Her mom turned off the stove. She set the wooden spoon in the sink. The worry lines deepened on her forehead as she blew out a sigh that lifted her permed bangs.

"Please don't try to talk me out of it." Clara left the kitchen before her mom could respond. Instead of backing away from a challenge like she usually did, Clara was ready to rise and meet it head on.

2. The Lonely Miles

"Clara, get in here, please." Her father's voice carried from his office with an edge of irritation.

She didn't want to move. The couch was so comfortable, and her legs were so stiff.

500-Mile Summer Challenge

Day 10: 5 miles complete

Total miles: 55

Not just her legs. Everything hurt: her back, her hips, her butt. The deep, aching pain surfaced in places she didn't even know could hurt. Movement made it worse. She wanted to lie on the couch and not move for the rest of the day.

"Clara." Her mom marched into the living room. "When your father calls, you answer him. Don't be disrespectful." She must've just touched up her hair because it was extra stiff and Clara smelled hairspray.

"I'm sorry," she whined. "I'm..." She was about to express her agony, but hesitated.

Her mom stood with her hands on her hips. The expression on her face with those raised eyebrows hinted at the "I told you so" she wanted to say. Maybe she was leaving that to Clara's father.

"I'm going." Clara labored to an upright, seated position on the couch. Her tender feet touched the carpet. As she stood, she worked to hide her discomfort, but each step toward the office sent ripples of muscle spasms and nerve shocks that made her wobble.

Classical music played softly from the stereo. "Shut the door, Clara." Her father sat in his swivel chair and gestured to the wooden one in the corner.

Clara didn't want to sit on the antique, but if she sat on the floor she might never get up again. She used the arms to lower herself gently onto her tender derriere.

Her father clasped his hands together and leaned forward in his chair. As he opened his mouth, a squeaking sound interrupted him. "Hang on a sec. I'm gonna grab the WD40." He rose and exited the room.

A moment of silence, and then one of Beethoven's symphonies played. She slouched in the uncomfortable chair, glancing at his computer. It was one of the newest IBM models. The screen was paused on a game of Frogger. A stack of floppy disks piled beside the monitor.

Dad returned with the WD40. He knelt, spraying the revolving parts of his chair. Seated again, he twisted and leaned. Nothing squeaked. He set the can on the desk. "You've been working too hard." When she opened her mouth to protest, her father's hand went up. "I can tell. I hate to see you putting so much pressure on yourself."

"It's not too much. Coach encouraged the whole team to do the challenge, and he's an expert."

"That may be. But, sweetie," his soft eyes saddened, "you're not as fast as those other kids."

"Exactly." Clara grinned. "That's why I'm doing this. I want to get better." Why couldn't her parents get excited about her persistence? Applaud her for being inspired to try something difficult? True, she might fail. Her body aches made it hard to get up in the mornings. Her Sunday rest days were precious and welcome. But it was all part of the challenge.

The symphony reached a crescendo.

"Beethoven." Clara gestured toward the stereo with her hand, one of the few body parts that didn't hurt. "He was deaf and created musical masterpieces!"

Her father exhaled through his nostrils. "What about all the limping around? This can't be good for your body."

"I'm not giving up. I just have to get used to it. That's all." Clara tried not to groan when she shifted in her seat. "I need to stretch more. That's my problem." The stretching helped somewhat with flexibility, but it didn't prevent the aches and pains.

"It seems like you could injure yourself. Why don't you come into it gradually?"

At least he wasn't dismissing her goal out of hand like Mom. "I won't be able to get all my miles in otherwise. It's five miles a day Monday through Friday, with ten miles on Saturday. I'll have to do 15 miles on my last few Saturdays. And that's accounting for every day of summer, so I can't skip a day or I won't make it."

Her dad cleared his throat. "I also don't like all this running you do by yourself."

A complaint she hadn't expected. "But our neighborhood is safe."

"Are you running only in our neighborhood?" he asked.

In order to log five miles, that would require twelve loops. Boring. "I'm running up Ocean Boulevard to the pier."

"That makes me uncomfortable. I've seen some sketchy characters around the pier."

"I just turn around and come back." After a bathroom break and sip of water from the fountain, which she didn't add. "There's hardly anyone there in the morning." An occasional sleeping bum, but they never bothered her.

"I wish you'd give up this challenge. You should be enjoying the summer, not beating yourself up. What about cutting the miles in half?"

Clara's heart sank into her throbbing toes. "You don't believe in me."

Her father tilted his head. "I'm sorry, Clara. It's not that. When I look at you, I fear you'll push yourself too hard. And I can't have you running to the pier by yourself." He stood up. "You can run with someone, but not by yourself."

She felt sentenced to prison. She wanted to scream about unfairness, but repressed the urge. "I'm seventeen."

"And you're my daughter living under my roof. I won't say anything else about the challenge. I can see your mind is made up. But I also can't make sure you'll stay in the neighborhood. Unless someone goes with you, you're not running."

3. Challenges

Her dad was being totally unfair. Should she go to her mom? No, she'd side with him. She probably gave him the idea in the first place. Even when she promised to run only in the neighborhood, he wouldn't budge. They were so overprotective. It was infuriating. She left his office with her face hot and her limbs shaky.

What could she do? She didn't have any friends who were runners, so her father's conditions were unbearable. Honestly, she never put much effort in during the off-season. Or in-season. This was her chance to prove to herself and to her parents that she didn't have to keep being average. Maybe she could even excel at this one thing. But not if they imposed stupid rules on her.

In her bedroom, she scanned the phone numbers of the cross country team. Missy and Paula ran together, but way too fast for her. They wouldn't want her bogging them down. Clara picked up the phone, twisting the long, curled cord around her finger. She called the two girls who might be willing to slow down to her pace. After hanging up, her shoulders sagged. Neither of them planned to do the summer challenge. They could only run with her twice a week.

She lay back on the bed, sinking into her feather pillow. Her pain mirrored what she felt inside. Her parents were so uptight and lame.

Downstairs, they were talking. Her mom raised her voice, making whatever they discussed sound more like an argument.

Clara rolled over onto her stomach. She pounded her fists into her pillow over and over. What was she supposed to do? Lie around doing nothing all summer? Her parents encouraged her *not* to get a job because it might be too stressful for her. They were the ones making her feel like she was stuffed inside a pressure cooker. She couldn't stay in the house another minute.

She picked up the phone and dialed the number for Danny's Breakfast Club. "Can I speak to Tyler Waller?" she asked the person who answered.

"Hullo?" Tyler always sounded like he just got out of bed, even in the middle of the day.

"Hey, it's Clara. Is Danny's hiring?"

"Why would you want to work here? Your parents don't make you have a job like mine do."

"Are they hiring or not?"

"I don't know. Pro'ly. Hang on." She heard clinking, chatter, and the far away voice of someone placing an order for eggs, bacon, and coffee. A scraping sound, and then Tyler was back. "Manager says they could use another waitress. If you wanna come by later."

"I'll be there in a few." Her dad couldn't object. It was a short walk through her neighborhood to Danny's—the opposite direction from the pier and in the nicer part of town. Until she got the job, she wouldn't bother her parents with details. She snuck downstairs and out the back door while they continued arguing in his study.

Ten minutes later at the old-fashioned bar, she glanced at a menu. She wasn't hungry, but she wanted to take a stab at memorizing the dishes. Danny's served breakfast all day, but also served lunch and dinner meals.

Tyler lumbered over and leaned his elbows on the counter. He smelled greasier than usual, like he applied the cooking oil as cologne. He wore an apron and a hair net. His overweight frame always made her sad. If only he'd start running, he could drop a few pounds and get healthier. But he was never interested.

"I'm not giving up the Atari, but I finally upgraded to Nintendo. Want to come over and play *Punch Out!!* tonight?"

"I'm not really in the mood for anything fun."

"I can see that." His large hand dwarfed hers as he pulled her fingers away from the menu. "Looks like a blue day," he said, tapping her mood ring.

"Almost black."

He nodded, letting her hand go. "I get it. Your parents don't want you to get a job, so you get one to spite them. Little rebel."

"I guess. But it's more than that. I hate feeling like there's nothing I'm good at, you know?"

"You got pretty good at *Pitfall!* in tenth grade. Too bad you don't come over and play much any more. You could be a video game queen."

"That's not what I want to be."

"You'd rather be a waitress." He raised a caterpillar eyebrow. "Whatever floats your boat."

She opened her mouth, about to explain. What she really wanted was to run 500 miles during the summer without stupid rules and limitations. Besides, getting a job meant she could save up for a car. A car meant more freedom.

The manager interrupted them. "You're Clara?" she asked in a high-pitched voice that sounded forced. "I'm Barb." The squat, baby-faced woman wore slacks and a button-up like the serving staff, but no apron. She shook Clara's hand. In Barb's other hand, she held a white sheet of paper. "Any experience?"

"No, but I'm willing and eager to learn."

"How old are you?"

"I'm seventeen. It's my summer break and I'd like to keep busy."

"Then you're hired, so long as your parents will sign this." She handed Clara the paper. "I could use another waitress for the two to ten shift. Will that work for you?"

Wow, that was easy. "Yes."

"Can you start tomorrow?"

"Sure. Thank you."

Tyler held the door open for Clara. "See you tomorrow, Speedy." He raised his palm, and she gave it a high five.

She skipped along the sidewalk. Waitressing could be fun. She secured the position without interference from her parents. Of course, she'd have to get their permission, but she'd find a way. The stiffening of her calves made her groan—a painful reminder of the challenge. At least she had one promising thing going for her: a summer job.

4. The Twilight Zone

Clara approached her house. An unfamiliar car was parked in the driveway.

The front door opened. Her mom peeked out and waved. "Where've you been?" Instead of the usual angst coupled with criticism, her mom had a smile and gestured for her to come in. "We've got some new friends to introduce you to."

"Who?" Clara asked, glancing back at the BMW.

Her mom opened the door all the way. A couple stood in the living room with their hands folded in front of them. Her mother might be mad that she'd left the house without saying anything, hiding the anger behind her hospitality smile.

"Mr. and Mrs. Palentino, I'd like you to meet our daughter, Clara."

She shook their hands. "Hi, call me Ron." The slick, dark hair and tan skin made Clara think Italian. His black leather jacket looked expensive.

"Oh, I'm so sorry, Dr. Palentino." Her mom covered her mouth. "I meant to say doctor, not mister."

He chuckled. "I prefer Ron. This is my wife, Ruth."

Ruth's perm was fluffier than Mom's. The jewelry around her neck and hanging from her ears looked heavy. "Nice to meet you, Clara," she said.

"You as well." Clara wasn't sure what to make of these people. Maybe they dropped by unexpectedly? How did her mom and dad know them, anyway?

"Here you are." Her father entered the room with two glasses of water, handing them out. Someone shadowed him, and it wasn't until Dad stepped aside that Clara got a good look at the teenager.

She held her own glass of water and sipped slowly. She was about Clara's height with wavy brunette hair. Yet something felt off about her. Something in her eyes.

"We'd like you to meet our daughter, Joan." Ron touched the girl's shoulder. She straightened up, unsmiling, her gaze aimed at the floor. Water sloshed out of her glass. "Oops. We're sorry," said Ron.

"It's nothing!" Mom said. "Just water. It'll dry right up."

"Joan, can you apologize for spilling?"

"Sorry, Mr. and Mrs. Boots." Her voice was monotone and a little too loud for their proximity. "I didn't mean to."

"Please, call me Doug. And it's okay. I'll grab a towel and it'll be good as new." Dad brought one out of the kitchen and dabbed the carpet. "No harm done."

Clara stared at her parents. Had she stepped into an episode of *The Twilight Zone*? They were acting weird. Mom hated when Clara spilled on the carpet. Of course, she wouldn't let strangers know that. Except these people were apparently their friends? From where? And something was up with this girl.

"Can you say hi to Clara?" Ruth prompted.

"Hi, Clara."

"Nice to meet you," she replied, glancing at her parents for some clue. They pasted on fake smiles.

"Reach out your hand and shake her hand. Okay, honey?" said Ron.

Joan had both hands on her water glass. She looked panicked, unsure how to accomplish the task. Was she mental or something?

Ruth gently took the water glass from her. "Go ahead."

Joan extended her arm. Clara reached out and shook Joan's stiff hand. The girl pulled it away. She never made eye contact with Clara.

"Well, this is wonderful," Mom said. "I'm so glad we could introduce you to our daughter. She's excited about this summer challenge. I bet Joan is, too."

The brakes squealed inside Clara's head. Summer challenge. Why would her mom bring that up?

Ruth addressed Clara. "We're thrilled that you're willing to run with Joan. It gives us such peace of mind. You must have amazing stamina like our daughter."

Clara's mind spun all the way to the ceiling. Were they talking about the same summer challenge? The 500-Mile Summer Challenge?

"She has been up every morning with only a break on Sundays," Dad said. "Since you all live in the neighborhood, it makes me far more comfortable about the whole thing. These girls can watch out for each other."

The puzzle pieces floated down from the ceiling and started taking shape on the floor where Clara's gaze had fallen. This was a set-up. They were going to make her run with this weird girl who probably couldn't make it around the block.

"We're heading to lunch with the pastor and his wife," said Ron. "We should go if we don't want to be late."

"I'll get those." Her mom collected the water glasses and took them to the kitchen.

"A pleasure, Clara. We'll be seeing you soon." Ron waved and walked out the door as Clara's dad held it open.

Ruth touched Clara's shoulder on the way out. "Thank you." Her eyes brimmed as if she was about to cry.

Clara forced a smile, nodding.

"Can you say goodbye?" asked Ron.

"Good-bye. Nice to meet you," Joan said as she rushed out the door behind her parents. Her awkward gait swung wide, each foot landing too far to the outside.

Her father waved to the three of them as they got into their car. "Bye! Enjoy your lunch."

Clara stared as the BMW pulled away. In the back seat, Joan dropped her chin. It was like a magnet kept it there. She wasn't normal.

Life was so unfair.

5. Blisters

"Clara, don't raise your voice." Her mother pointed her finger as a warning.

"Fine. I'll calmly tell you that I can't believe you."

Her father wrapped an arm around her mother's shoulder. "Clara, your mother found someone for you to run with. You should thank her for being so considerate."

"But I can't run with that girl. Isn't she retarded or something?"

"Don't say that word," her mom scolded.

"It's not a swear word."

"Well, it could be seen as offensive by some people."

"What people? We're the only ones here. I'm not calling her a retard to her face."

"Clara." Her mom's hand went over her mouth. "That's unkind."

"Joan has no mental retardation," her dad said. "She struggles with social skills, like her parents mentioned."

When did they say that? What was Clara missing? "They had to show her everything to do. Even then she didn't seem like she could handle the situation. How are we supposed to run every day when she can barely hold a glass of water without spilling it? I know I'm slow, but not *that* slow."

"Clara." Again that gaze of disbelief from her mother. "This isn't like you. You're usually so accepting of people."

"I'm sure Joan's great. But you're the ones who are forcing me to run with someone. I like running alone. I didn't ask to be paired up. Especially not with a girl who can't make it one mile, let alone 500. How did you even find those people?"

"I see." Her mother nodded, some bulb of understanding clicking on. "Doug, we haven't explained anything to her. This is our fault, Clara. Sit and we'll tell you everything."

She obeyed, plopping back onto the couch and wrapping her arms around a pillow. Whatever they said, Clara didn't plan on removing her scowl.

"We met the Palentinos at church on Sunday. I completely forgot you weren't there with us," her mom said.

After all her early morning runs, Clara had begged off church for extra sleep. Her parents had reluctantly agreed.

"They shared with us that Joan had a brain injury when she was younger, which is why she struggles with social skills now."

A brain injury. That explained her struggle with simple tasks like drinking water and engaging with strangers.

"She's at a special education school because of her social issues," her mom continued. "It was too difficult for her in a regular middle and high school, but she's taking advanced math and science classes through a dual enrollment college program. She has straight A's."

Clara cleared her throat. "At her special ed school."

"No, in the college courses. She's very smart," her father chimed in.

"And she runs cross country," Mom said. "There is no official team, but she trains at the school track. Her parents think she doesn't mind going in circles, but they've been wondering if she would enjoy running elsewhere where she might get more out of it."

"Something you guys obviously don't want for me."

"Now, Clara, your mother pointed out to me that I might've been a tad unfair, but she also has her concerns when it comes to you running alone."

Clara stared at her mother, the scowl fading. Mom said that to Dad? That must've been what they had argued about when she snuck out of the house.

"Your mom suggested that if we put this stipulation on you, then we should create a solution. Immediately, we thought of Joan as the perfect partner. Not just for your sake, but for hers, too. She doesn't have many friends."

Clara could relate to that. She felt a softening in her heart toward the girl. But would Joan be able to keep up? "I know I'm not fast. But do you know anything about Joan's pace?"

Her dad frowned. "I'm not sure. We figured you two could find a comfortable one together."

It wasn't that simple. Clara never thought she'd need to slow down for someone else. Suddenly she understood her teammates' aversion to running with a slower partner. The idea of taking longer to finish the miles didn't appeal to her.

"Will you at least give her a chance?" Her mom's pleading eyes locked on Clara's ankle. "What would Jesus do?"

Clara glanced at the colorful anklet she had braided while volunteering with the fifth graders at Sunday School. One side had white stitching that spelled *WWJD?* She honestly hadn't thought about it. "You know you cornered me, right? I had no idea who those people were or what they were doing here until Joan's mom said she was grateful that I agreed to run with her. Which I didn't."

"I guess I got a little ahead of myself. I'm sorry," Mom apologized.

"Remember, Clara, if you don't have anyone to run with, I'm sticking to my guns. I don't want you out there alone," said Dad.

"Yeah, I remember." How could she forget? They left her with no options.

"It's a great compromise," he said. "You can do your challenge with someone, and we'll feel better about your safety. And I think God would have you show kindness to Joan."

Clara didn't want to be mean, but she wasn't crazy about being stuck with the awkward girl. Missy and Paula would make fun of Clara just for being around someone like Joan. Not that she cared about their opinions. She didn't have any popularity to lose.

More importantly, she wouldn't complete the challenge without a running partner, and right now Joan was it.

"Tomorrow, I'll go with her. But I can't promise more than that."

6. The Turtle and the Tortoise

At six o'clock in the morning, Clara stood outside one of the nicest houses in the neighborhood. The cinnamon-colored Spanish-style was accented with a coffee brown trim. Joan's dad was a doctor and obviously made a lot of money. The three-car garage to the right implied two more luxury vehicles to go along with the BMW.

The sunrise meant the air would only stay cool for a little while longer. Clara needed to stop wasting time. She knocked.

When the door opened, Ruth greeted her with a lipstick-free smile. She wore a fluffy pink bathrobe with matching slippers. Even though she wore no makeup, her hair looked styled and as big as the day before. "Hi, Clara. Would you like to come in?"

"Okay." She crossed the threshold into an elegantly decorated entryway that opened into a large living area. Most of the furniture was pearly white and looked brand new.

The place even smelled expensive, like the perfumes her mother suggested she not touch at the mall lest she break one and have to buy it.

"Thank you," said Ruth. "This means so much to us."

Clara clamped her lips together as she lifted a half-smile. "Sure." She hated to disappoint Dr. and Mrs. Palentino, but in reality, she was worse than a reluctant partner. This run would determine whether or not she'd be on a desperate hunt this afternoon to find someone else.

"Do you need a bottle of water? Or to use the restroom before your run?" Ruth asked.

"No, I'm fine." But something else occurred to Clara. "Do I need to do anything? To…help her?" She almost said, *hold her hand*, but if Joan ran circles at the track, she probably didn't need hand holding.

"Oh." Ruth touched her finger to her lips, tapping. "We've already told her to stay right at your side, and she will. She won't wander off or anything. She's a good runner, so she should keep up. And we've told her to follow your lead and instructions about where to go on the route. If she needs the restroom, she'll tell you."

Clara didn't want to ask whether or not Joan needed help in the ladies' room. Ruth probably would've mentioned that. "There's a bathroom at the pier, so I'll make sure we stop there."

"Wonderful. Joan?" Ruth called upstairs. "Are you ready?"

Someone stomped down the hardwood steps. Joan appeared with one shoe untied. She held the bannister with both hands.

"Here, let me help you. Sit right there." When her mother spoke, Joan obeyed. She sat a few steps up from Ruth with her feet planted on the lowest stair. Ruth retied and double-knotted the laces. "There."

Joan stood and approached Clara with her head down. Her hair was pulled back into a ponytail. She wore stylish pink Guess shorts with a cute matching running top that looked like a modern artist splattered pink and purple paint on it. Clara longed for cute running outfits, but her mom always made her get workout clothes from thrift shops since they were "just for sweating in," as she put it.

"You and Clara will have a great time on your five miles. Five, right?" Ruth confirmed with a glance at Clara.

"Yeah." Except she'd be amazed if they made it past one.

"And you'll stay together like we talked about."

Joan nodded.

Clara imagined the usual fifty or so minutes would end up doubled. She had no choice. It was extra slow or nothing at all. "We'll jog to the pier and back. I'll make sure we stay together."

"Bless you," she whispered. "Now off you go. Have fun!"

The walk outside gave Clara the distinct impression that Joan took commands literally. She stuck to Clara's right side like glue. That could be a good sign. Clara dared to hope that she'd keep up. "I stretched at home. Did you stretch?"

Joan shook her head no.

"Oh." Clara realized she should take the lead and make sure she wasn't the reason Joan pulled a muscle. "Let's do a few here in the grass." Might as well take the time. It was going to be a long morning.

Joan had difficulty holding any of the stretching poses. She tipped over into the grass a few times, but didn't act embarrassed or concerned. She was nowhere near reaching her toes, but then again Clara had little flexibility before a run.

"Let's get this over with." Clara covered her mouth, not meaning to say that out loud.

Joan's immovable mask remained in place. If she felt anything—hurt or anticipation—she didn't show it. She lined up on the sidewalk next to Clara.

With a few walking steps, Joan matched Clara stride for stride. They went around the block and Clara picked up the pace to a slow jog. Again, Joan remained in sync with her. For now, Clara decided to keep the pace very slow.

They wound through the neighborhood in a steady rhythm. Although it took longer to reach Ocean Boulevard, Clara thought this might be difficult for Joan and worked at not pushing her any faster. They both ran alone and, like Clara, Joan probably preferred it that way. They said nothing as they passed the mile marker—the golden arches of McDonald's.

What could they talk about anyway? Clara had no idea how to relate to Joan. She pitied her, and felt sorry that she had judged her harshly yesterday. Her mother was right about Clara's unkindness. Her face burned.

At two miles, Joan kept up without complaint. She didn't run in the same awkward way she got around the rest of the time. Joan had a natural gait that made running look effortless.

Clara had to work at it and knew her gait looked labored. Most of the time, her legs felt as heavy as watermelons. Her stinging lungs gave her the impression she inhaled less than half the oxygen she required. She was often one step away from quitting. That was why she'd never pushed herself. It was already hard and she'd had little motivation to improve before now. At this slower pace, she breathed in and out with little difficulty. Her legs felt strong for the first time since she'd started the challenge. For once, she could focus on good form and not just survival.

With plenty of air flow, Clara racked her brain for conversation starters. "Do you like music?"

"I like music that has no talking."

It took Clara a moment to process whether or not Joan meant the statement as an insult. The lack of inflection in her speech made it difficult to interpret. Was she trying to say she wanted no talking during the run? Or was she simply stating she liked instrumental music? Joan's expression remained unchanged. She didn't exactly frown. It was more like a constant pout. Clara had yet to see her smile, and the mask had only fallen when Joan seemed nervous.

Clara went with the instrumental interpretation. "My dad listens to classical music like Bach, Handel, and Beethoven."

"Yes." Joan's pout relaxed, but not into a smile. More like a straight-lipped line.

"You like classical?"

"Yes," she repeated. "It's nice."

"Yeah," Clara agreed. "I do like other music, too, like Bananarama, New Kids on the Block, the Eurythmics, and Cyndi Lauper. But their songs have talking."

"Yes."

They stopped at the intersection before the pier waiting for cars to pass. The fumes from a large truck speeding through left a haze that Clara wasn't excited to pass through. They got a whiff of exhaust as they headed for the restroom. "I'm going to the bathroom. Do you need to?"

"Okay."

A homeless man slept on a nearby bench. No one had ever bothered Clara before, but she acknowledged that having a partner was a good idea. As they walked in together, Joan didn't pant like Clara expected. She wasn't even sweating much. Wisps of hair framed her face. She looked energized, except the pout was still in place.

Clara glanced back when Joan disappeared from her peripheral.

Joan had both hands pressed against the wall at the step that led down into the bathroom. She lifted one foot timidly.

"Do you need help?" Clara reached out a hand remembering how Joan came downstairs holding the rail.

Joan slid her palms down the wall, bracing herself. "I don't."

"Okay." Clara stayed close anyway.

With her leg extended, Joan twisted her body closer to the wall. She lowered the foot until it touched the ground. Both hands slid with her movement until she cleared the step without incident.

After Clara washed her hands, she stood at the step waiting to see if Joan needed help up. Out of the stall, she walked toward Clara.

"Um. Be sure to wash your hands."

Joan obeyed.

"Let's get a drink from the fountain. Then we'll head home."

Joan nodded.

Clara stepped up slowly. Joan mimicked her and easily climbed the single stair and followed Clara out to the boardwalk. Maybe it was only going down that gave Joan difficulty.

The cold fountain cooled Clara's lips and throat. She took one long drink and stopped. Too much water would slosh around in her stomach and make her uncomfortable on the way back. Like Joan had done with everything else, she followed Clara's example and drank for about five seconds before releasing the button.

The salty sea air met the sweat on Clara's skin. She loved the cool breeze washing over her. Seagulls passed overhead. White droppings splashed the boardwalk near Joan.

"Ew."

Clara giggled. "I'm glad it didn't hit you."

"Me, too."

The sun hovered above the horizon, giving the ocean a tint of yellow streaks. Waves lazily crashed against the sand. Up the boardwalk, the pier stretched out half a mile over the water. Silhouettes fished off the sides. "It's beautiful, isn't it?" Clara remarked.

"Yes."

Something on Joan's neck drew Clara's gaze. A small scar near the base of her throat. Clara wondered about it, but didn't feel comfortable probing.

With their backs to the picturesque scene, Clara said, "Let's cross the road." No cars were in sight, and they resumed the steady jog back toward home.

Ruth greeted them at the open front door with a red smile. Some of her lipstick smeared on her teeth. She wore a patterned black and white dress with matching bangles and earrings. "How did it go?"

"The run was great." Clara was surprised to hear herself say it, but it was true. She didn't feel as much heaviness in her legs as usual. Her heart beat a strong rhythm. Each breath filled her lungs. She hadn't had a run so satisfying in a long time. If ever. Sure, it took longer, but only twenty-five extra minutes.

"Joan, you stayed with Clara?"

"Yes." She nodded, and Clara detected the hint of a smile. But maybe she imagined it. Joan had a light dusting of salty sweat on her skin, but otherwise looked ready to run another five miles.

The arrangement Clara's parents had forced upon her turned out to be better than she ever could have imagined.

She didn't have to hunt for someone else. Not yet, at least. So long as Joan could keep pace, Clara would be happy to have her as a partner. The revelation made all her pouting and complaining an embarrassment.

If Joan became too exhausted from six days of running each week, Clara could try a day or two with the other cross country girls. And then there was the longer mileage to consider on Saturdays. "I'd better head home. Tomorrow is the ten-mile day. Is that cool with you, Joan?"

Joan stared at the floor, reminding Clara of their awkward introduction the day before.

"Yes, she'll be ready to go right at six," Ruth answered for her. "Joan, can you say, 'See you then?'"

"See you then. Goodbye."

"Bye." Clara waved and jogged the two blocks to her house.

Her mom opened the door. "Forget something?" She dangled the spare key over Clara's head.

"Yes. But I knew you'd be home anyway." Clara breezed past her mom and stepped out of her running shoes.

"So?"

Clara didn't turn around. She slipped off her damp socks and put them in her shoes.

"How was it?"

Her mom could suffer through some minor anxiety before getting an answer. "Well...if every day goes like today…" Clara glanced over her shoulder, "then I'm pretty sure I'll complete the challenge with Joan."

"Really?" Mom made fists over her heart and shook them like maracas. The tic of excitement used to bother Clara, but she'd gotten used to her mother's weirdness.

"Joan is nice. She doesn't talk much, but she keeps up."

"I'm glad this worked out." Her mom lowered her arms and slouched her shoulders. "I hope you're not too upset about the way your father and I handled the situation."

"I'm not upset." Clara could appreciate her mom's remorse. And it gave her the opportunity to broach the subject of her summer job. "But I do have something I need you to do for me."

"Oh? What's that?"

"Hold on." Clara dashed upstairs to her room where the paper sat under a notebook on her desk. The night before, she had filled out everything herself. A signature was the only thing missing. She brought it to her mom. "I got a job waitressing at Danny's. And I need you to sign off."

"What?" Her mom stared without comprehension before accepting the paper. She read it.

"Mom, I ran with Joan for you and Dad. Please do this for me. I'm going to start saving money so I can get a car. You guys won't buy me one, and I understand. But that means you should support me when I want a job to pay for one myself. Besides, it's walking distance in a nice area," Clara pointed out.

Her mom's gaze lifted from the paper. Her lips broke apart and she laughed. "When did you become so grown up?"

A loud sigh escaped from Clara. "Many years ago."

A deep guffaw erupted from the office.

Sometimes her dad worked from home. She had no idea he'd been listening in, but she took that as a yes.

7. The First Few Hundred Miles

500-Mile Summer Challenge

Day 20: 2 miles to complete

Total miles: 113

"Do you like running around the track?" Clara asked.

Joan nodded. "I like it."

They jogged the same turtle pace as the previous ten days. Clara couldn't imagine going this slow in circles for five miles, let alone ten. "I have to admit, I like running off track better." She glanced over her shoulder, back at the pier and the rising sun. "The sights can be beautiful." They had stopped for their usual bathroom and water break less than a mile ago. "Do you like running this route, too?"

"Yes."

"I'm glad." She'd hate for Joan to be miserable on the daily runs. To think, Clara had only been concerned about herself when her parents first set her up with her running partner. "So Danny's is pretty hard work. But it's only for the summer. Getting a paycheck is the best part." Clara and Tyler cracked jokes in the back, but only during slow times. She made sure the customers were taken care of first. Being attentive to their needs gave her something to do that kept her legs moving. It released some of the lactic acid that built up every day during the run. "Have you ever eaten at Danny's?"

"Yes."

"Do you like it?"

"Yes. It's good."

"What do you like?"

"Waffles."

"With strawberries and whipped cream on top? That's my favorite, too."

"Yummy."

The next mile went on in silence. Clara had an idea. They'd been consistent in their pacing, why not speed up at the end? Joan could probably handle it. She waited, guessing where the final 800 meters began. She slowly increased the pace. Joan stayed in her peripheral, but didn't come up to meet her. Clara pulled ahead, but then she couldn't see Joan at all. She twisted to look over her shoulder.

As if stuck in the slower pace, Joan frowned deeper than her usual pout. Clara pulled back. "I was thinking we could speed up. Is that okay? We've been running the same pace for a while now. Might be good to end the run a little faster."

"Okay." The frown remained, but Joan followed this time when Clara increased the speed.

They jogged a little faster than Clara's old pace, ending the run at a good clip in front of Joan's house.

"Nice job." Clara raised her hand. "How about a high five?"

Only when prompted with words would Joan raise her arm. She posed with her hand over her shoulder like someone being sworn in at court.

Clara gently slapped her palm into Joan's. "See you to-morrow."

"See you tomorrow. Goodbye."

In the days that followed, Clara made it a habit of speeding up during the last 800 meters, even on the ten miler. Joan always kept up. Verbal commands went a long way with her.

The next week, Clara decided to try something else. She'd been pacing them nice and slow, and then adding a strong 800-meter finish. Why not speed up the regular pacing a little bit to see if Joan could handle it?

They started at the turtle pace and made it to the Mc-Donald's mile marker before Clara brought it up. "Joan, I'm thinking about speeding up the pace today. What do you think?"

"Not at four and a half miles yet," she answered.

She must've gotten used to their routine. Clara tried again. "I mean, what if we speed up the pace for the rest of the run starting now?"

"No."

The answer was quick, delivered in that same monotone that made Joan sound sure about everything she said.

"We could try it out and see?"

"No."

Clara didn't press the issue. This pace must be all Joan could handle. Clara would hate to feel pushed by someone like Missy or Paula. Had they been her running partners, Clara wouldn't have lasted more than a week. Their pace could probably kill her, not to mention the horrible gossiping she would have to endure.

500-Mile Summer Challenge
Day 52: 1 mile to complete
Total miles: 299

Another milestone right around the corner: 300 miles. They were almost back to Joan's house. All this time, and

Clara hadn't once thought about searching for another running partner since that first day with Joan. A little slower speed didn't hurt. In fact, it seemed to help decrease soreness. Clara might not have lasted at the rate she'd been going. It was pretty ridiculous that she could barely walk before. No wonder her parents had been concerned. With Joan needing to keep things slower, she kept Clara accountable to the turtle pace.

They reached the invisible finish line in front of Joan's house.

"Three hundred miles. Woohoo! High five." Clara's hand met Joan's. "You're a great running partner."

"Thank you," she said, her gaze dropping into the grass.

"Have you always liked running?" Clara asked.

"No."

"Your school doesn't have a team. What made you start?"

Joan shifted her weight back and forth. She rubbed her hands together in front of her as if washing them under an imaginary faucet. Clara had never seen her do that before.

"When did you start running?"

Again, no answer. Joan took a step backward.

"In middle school? High school? Before that?"

Joan turned around and shuffled toward the front door. She disappeared into the house, leaving Clara dumbfounded on the lawn. She'd never done that before. But then again, Clara always left right after they finished the jog. Maybe this was an uncomfortable break in Joan's routine.

Clara headed home thinking about what she might've done to make Joan run away. It could be as simple as her inability to socialize. Clara didn't ask Joan many personal questions. Maybe her brain injury kept her from processing those kinds of things.

In the future, she'd try to avoid upsetting her.

8. Potholes

Missy and Paula breezed into Danny's and slid into a booth. Their hair was tousled and sprayed like Madonna's in her latest music video. Bangles encircled their wrists and they wore large hoop earrings. Their clothing style matched, too, with off the shoulder slouchy tees and cut-off jean shorts.

Missy blew a large bubble with her gum and popped it when she noticed Clara. "I didn't know you worked here."

"Just for summer."

"Hey," said Paula. Her dark blue eyeshadow gave her eyes a beady look. "I've seen you, like, running with that retarded girl."

Clara's fingers tightened around the handle of the coffee pot she held. "Joan isn't retarded."

"Oh, yeah." Missy snapped her gum. "That's that girl who got kidnapped. She has damage to the brain."

Kidnapped? Clara didn't know anything about Joan's injury. How did Missy know about it?

"Brain damage, retarded, same thing. I'm surprised her parents let her out of the house." Paula tapped her long nails on the menu. "Can I get a burger and fries with a Coke?"

"Same here. I'm starved. We've been running, like, twenty miles a week all summer."

A burning heat filled Clara's nostrils. "Joan and I run thirty-five a week. We're up to 450 miles. Just fifty to go and we'll have completed the summer challenge."

Missy stopped smacking her gum. She and Paula gaped at Clara.

"That brain-damaged girl runs with you every day?" asked Paula, a stank look on her face. "How do you put up with her?"

Clara imagined splashing them both with the hot coffee. She took a deep breath. *WWJD.* "I don't know what you mean."

"It's for charity, right? You're getting volunteer hours. Good for you." Missy clapped, but her hands barely touched.

"She's my friend," Clara growled. "And she has all A's in her college courses, so she's a lot smarter than any of us." She didn't mean to let her anger slip, but that shut them up. "I'll put your order in."

As she walked to the kitchen, Clara knew she had become their gossip target for senior year. But she didn't care about that. She wanted them to stop bad-mouthing Joan.

"Don't let them get to you." Tyler dropped two frozen patties onto the grill. They sizzled alongside the other burgers. "Should I spit in their food?"

"Ew. No. But I appreciate the support."

He flipped the patties that had cooked through. "Any time."

The kidnapping. How had Clara never heard about that? She'd never asked what led to Joan's injury. Clara wanted to know more, but she wouldn't ask Missy or Paula. Not Joan, either. She didn't want to upset her. She'd have to get answers from someone else.

9. The Missing Days

In a modern and updated kitchen, Ruth filled a glass with ice and Coke and set it in front of Clara. The sweet, floral aroma of Ruth's perfume wafted through the room. "Joan and her dad are at the store, but they should be home soon."

Clara accepted the glass and took a sip. The bubbles fizzled down her throat. "It's actually you that I came to talk to, Mrs. Palentino."

"Oh?" She scratched her neck with long, red nails.

"I was wondering about Joan. What—what happened to her?"

Ruth inhaled and her chest heaved. She moved toward one of the barstools, lowering slowly. With hands clasped on the counter and a glance at the front door, she exhaled. "When she was eight years old, Joan was taken from us."

So it was true. She was kidnapped. "Some girls from school—" Clara clenched her jaw. "I didn't like the way they were talking about Joan. I thought maybe they were just gossiping. Was it in the paper?"

Ruth blinked, exhaling through her nostrils. "It made the local news."

When Clara was eight, her family lived in another state. They moved when she turned ten, two years after the incident. That must be why she'd never heard about it.

"We hired a contractor to do work on a house we used to live in. One day, he took Joan right out of her bedroom." Ruth's clasped hands trembled. She squeezed them, firming up her grip. "He'd barely started on the work. Both my husband and I were discussing something in our room upstairs. We were arguing, so my husband shut the door. Joan's room was on the first floor. She'd been playing with her dolls and listening to a record. It never occurred to us…" A tear rolled down her cheek as Ruth stared out the window. "She was missing for a week."

What a horrible ordeal for Joan, not to mention her parents. "I'm so sorry, Mrs. Palentino."

Ruth lifted her cheeks in an attempt to smile, but her sad eyes continued to dampen her face with tears. "You've been a wonderful friend to Joan. It's been such a blessing to her and to us."

"She's been one to me, too," Clara said. "What led to the brain damage?"

"He shot her in the head."

The words struck Clara in the same way the gun must've exploded in a sudden flash. How had Joan survived?

"And he left her body in a dumpster." Ruth dabbed her eyes with a napkin. "Someone found her. She was rushed to a hospital where my husband's colleagues saved her life."

Clara had no idea someone could survive after being shot in the head.

"They said she would be a vegetable, and that we should end her life support. But we knew God had a plan. We told them to do everything they could for her. After two months in a coma, she woke up. Even though she couldn't talk at the time, it was more than any of the doctors had expected."

"That mark." Clara touched the base of her throat where she had seen Joan's scar. "What happened there?"

"That's from a tube they put in at the hospital while she was in the coma. Once she came out of it, rehabilitation was slow. It took her a year to learn how to walk and talk again. In that time, she demonstrated that her intelligence was intact. She'd always been smart. But due to where the bullet lodged, she continues to struggle with social skills and communication, as you know."

The more time Clara spent with Joan, the more she saw her as a girl who simply didn't talk much. So she had some struggles figuring out how to act around people. Didn't everyone in one circumstance or another? "Why is she afraid of going down stairs?"

Ruth shrugged. "There's a lot we don't know. We think he might have kept her in a basement. Stairs could be a subconscious trigger according to her therapist. The man was never apprehended, and police think he fled the country. The hospital found…evidence of abuse." Ruth looked like she tasted a raw lemon. "Thankfully, Joan doesn't remember any of it." She blew her nose. "I think that's God sparing her from whatever she went through."

Clara couldn't believe it. How could someone do that to a little girl? And then he tried to kill her.

But Joan was strong. She had survived and now thrived in a way no one predicted. "You saved her life, too, by not giving up."

"I'll never give up on her."

"Me either."

Ruth blinked, a genuine smile forming that brightened her eyes. "You know, she's been more talkative since she met you. At least at home. Her therapist hasn't noticed much change in their sessions. But I'm hopeful."

That surprised Clara considering the few words Joan spoke to her. "I do most of the talking when we jog, but I'm really glad to hear that. When did she start running?"

"During rehabilitation. Once she could walk again, she could run. And she loved running on the treadmill."

Clara finished the Coke and set the glass down. "Thank you for sharing with me. And for the drink."

"You're welcome. It's kind of you to show interest in her. So many young people don't understand her and don't want to take the effort to try like you have. We're so grateful."

Initially, Clara had been guilty of that, too. She judged Joan before she knew her. Which gave her an idea. "Mrs. Palentino, may I ask you one last question?"

10. Mission's End

On their final challenge day, Clara jogged into the opening mile with Joan at her side. She couldn't believe how fast the summer flew by. Had she attempted to complete the 500 miles on her own, an injury or mental exhaustion would've benched her. Thanks to Joan and their turtle pace, she'd been able to push through every step.

Because Clara started ten days earlier than Joan, she had considered adding some mileage to make sure Joan completed the full amount as well. She found out from Ruth that Joan ran the extra miles on her own while her dad rode alongside her on a bicycle.

The ten-mile route initially led them the opposite direction of Ocean Boulevard toward Danny's Breakfast Club. They wound through neighborhoods and eventually made their way back to the pier with two and a half miles to go. After the bathroom and water break, Clara asked if they could admire the view. She needed the extra minute of rest. If she'd learned anything, it was the ability to persist in the midst of discomfort.

As Clara leaned against the boardwalk railing soaking in the salty air, Joan mimicked her, gazing out over the water toward the horizon. Clara couldn't help it. She searched for Joan's hidden scars. Her silky brunette hair was pulled into her usual ponytail, covering up any evidence. The sunbeams showed hints of reddish highlights. Mrs. Palentino had said that she styled Joan's hair in a way that covered over the scar even when she left it down.

"We're almost done with the 500-Mile Summer Challenge. Do you think we can keep being running partners after this?"

Joan's gaze lowered toward the beach below them. "Yes. Partner."

The simple answer pleased Clara. She imagined that if Joan could express excitement, she would have. "I have another question for you. And you can think about it. You don't have to answer right away." She reordered the phrasing in her mind, hoping to make herself clear to Joan. "At my school, we have a cross country team. I'm usually by myself in the back when I run with them. At your school, I know you have to run alone on the track. So I asked my coach and he said you could come run with me when practice starts next week. Would you like to do that?"

"Yes. Yes. I would like it. Yes."

Clara leaned back in amazement, hanging onto the rail. That must be what enthusiasm looked like for Joan. "I was hoping you'd say that." For another minute, Clara took in the ocean scene. A light breeze cooled her skin. Only a few more miles to the end. "Let's finish this."

They left the pier, the sun at their backs. Clara was beyond exhaustion, but with Joan's help, she knew they'd make it. The last half mile at the faster pace took them all the way home.

"We did it!" Clara high-fived Joan. She collapsed into the grass panting. Joan awkwardly lowered herself into the yard beside her. They laid on their backs gazing up at the blue sky.

"Hey!" Mr. Palentino came out of the house with bottled water. "Way to go, girls. You did 500 miles in one summer."

Clara sat up and gratefully accepted the drink. "We did. Together."

"Together," Joan echoed.

One challenge was over, and another would begin.

11. The Cross Country Team

Clara's mom dropped her and Joan off at the park where the cross country team met for practice. A city worker drove a riding lawn mower nearby. A wide sidewalk encircled the outer edge of the park. Two laps on the grass just inside that sidewalk equaled three point one miles, or five kilometers. Home meets for their 5K races would take place there.

A welcome cloud cover prevented the sun from baking their skin. The opening of the season was always the hardest with the warmer weather. Clara couldn't wait until it cooled down. They stood on the sidewalk while the rest of the team huddled in a group on the grass. Clara knew how much more of an outsider she would be now that Joan was with her, but she didn't care. When the loud mower moved away, Clara pulled a slip of paper out of her pocket. "I almost forgot. This is for you. It's something Coach said, and it encouraged me when I needed it."

Joan took the paper and read what Clara had written.

Today is the first day of the rest of your life.

"My life today." Joan put the paper in her pocket.

Whatever her words meant, Clara was pretty sure Joan appreciated what Clara had given her. "I'm glad you're here with me, Joan."

"I'll be glad when we run."

Joan must be nervous. Clara could relate. "Me, too."

They walked toward the cross country team together while the eight others stared. Clara hoped it didn't upset Joan.

"Great to have you with us." Coach McFarland approached and shook both of their hands. "Everyone, this is Joan. Say hello."

A few weak hellos came from the group. Missy and Paula whispered to each other. Clara ignored them.

"She'll be joining us for practice," said Coach. "And I hope some meets, too."

Clara turned to her excitedly. "You could compete, Joan. Would you like to do that?"

She stared at her feet. "Yes."

"I understand that Clara and Joan are the only ones who have completed the 500-Mile Summer Challenge. Congratulations are in order." Coach clapped, and everyone followed his example. "I'm really proud of you two. I know it wasn't easy. Your tremendous persistence will pay off this season, I'm sure of it."

Feeling honored, Clara grinned at Joan, who continued staring at the ground. No one else had done it? That alone should make them show Joan her due respect.

"All right, then. Let's get started."

The slow warm-up mile was a nice and easy jog. As the coach gave instructions, Clara provided Joan with more details, and, of course, they stayed together. But they weren't in the back. It was obvious who hadn't been running during the summer.

"To end our practice, I'll be timing each of you for a 5K in two groups of five," Coach said. "Those who can finish in under 22 minutes will be competing at the invitational next weekend. The rest will be expected to attend in support of your teammates. Our first official meet will be in two weeks."

The first group included Missy, Paula, and the three fastest boys on the team. Coach sent them off with a countdown, clicking one of the stopwatches around his neck. They sprinted away at an incredibly fast pace that Clara could only match in her dreams.

After they had gone about halfway around the park, he lined up the second group. Before Clara could give Joan any instructions, Coach spoke directly to her. "Joan, will you be comfortable running at your own pace this time, and not with Clara? I'd like to see what you can do if you're racing without her, but only if that's okay with you."

Clara felt inclined to add, "You can run whatever your fastest speed would be for a 5K distance. Don't worry about staying with me, just run two laps around the park as fast as you can. Is that okay?"

"Yes. Run like it's a race."

"Exactly."

Clara wasn't sure how fast Joan would be on her own, but she didn't anticipate the immediate sprint that launched Joan ahead of their group as soon as Coach said, "Go." To Clara's surprise, Joan widened the gap with no indicators that she would slow down.

After the consistent five-mile daily grind with ten and fifteen miles thrown in, Clara pushed herself as hard as she could for the 5K. Her body responded with strength and stamina. The first lap passed quickly with a pleasant wind that didn't hinder her forward motion. Coach read, *"12:05,"* off his stopwatch when she passed him. That was the best time Clara had ever gotten on a first lap. Only one of the three other teammates had passed her. She wasn't last.

By the time Clara started lap two, Joan was already more than halfway through it and nearing the finish. Clara had no idea that Joan could run so fast. All summer, she thought of the turtle pace as Joan's pace. Clara couldn't make twenty-two minutes, but could Joan?

As she rounded the curve and headed back toward Coach, she could see Joan standing beside him. Clara's curiosity overwhelmed her. She had to get back and find out Joan's time. She didn't hear what Coach said about her own time when she crossed the finish. She ran up to Joan. "What was your time?"

"Twenty."

"Twenty minutes?" She gaped, and then turned to Coach. He nodded, calling out times to the last two girls finishing.

Panting, Clara squeezed Joan's shoulders. "Wow! Why didn't you tell me you were so fast?"

"You needed slow for summer," she stated with even breaths. Her skin glistened, hardly a droplet on her. "To finish challenge."

The sweat pouring down Clara's forehead threatened to sting her eyes. She wiped her brow with the back of her hand, biting her lip. All that time, she thought she'd been pacing for Joan. But it was the other way around.

"Nice job, Joan." One of the boys, Lenny Johnson, passed her and winked. "You were the fastest girl."

Joan's eyes widened as she thrust her chin down to her chest, focusing on her shoes as she so often did.

Clara glanced at Missy and Paula. The girls secluded themselves by a tree, folding their arms and pouting. "I had no idea you slowed down so much for me," she said to Joan. "Thank you for that."

"Good for me, too."

"Nice job, you guys," said Coach. "Six of you will be competing at the invitational. Lenny, Jack, Patrick, Missy, Paula, and Joan. I expect the rest of you to join me in the stands."

Clara beamed, slipping her arm through Joan's. They walked to her mom's car where she waited in the parking lot. "Mom, you won't believe what happened."

12. A New Season

At the invitational, Clara's parents and Joan's parents sat together in the bleachers behind Clara and the cross country team. She wore the t-shirt her mom had helped her make with Joan's name and number on it.

The female competitors approached the starting line on the track. Clara wished she could go down to give Joan support, but the rules wouldn't allow it before the race. They'd talked a lot that day about what Joan should do.

"Just like our practices, you'll be running mostly in the grass. And you won't be alone," Clara had explained. "The other girls will be trying to get ahead of you, but you do your best to stay near the front of the pack."

"I might throw up," Joan had admitted. "Embarrassing."

"If you do, it's okay. Just run the best race you can. That's all."

Clara felt nervous for her as Joan stood amongst strangers at the starting line. Missy and Paula placed themselves closer to the inside lane. They couldn't be bothered to stand with their teammate.

God, please help Joan.

The gun fired. The girls dashed into the first corner. Joan pressed in with the front runners, landing in third place as they merged together into the first lane. One lap around the track, and then they followed the cones that led out into the wide open cross country course. Clara kept her eyes on Joan as long as she could. The group disappeared one by one into a wooded area where they would complete most of the race. Joan had kept up with the front runners so far, but she had over two miles to go.

Clara hated not knowing what was happening. Suddenly, she understood her mom's struggle with anxiety. Clara glanced over her shoulder. Higher up in the bleachers, Mom and Dad grinned down at her. Dr. Palentino gave her a thumbs up, and Mrs. Palentino nodded with a worried expression. She was suffering the same agony as Clara.

Some of the fastest runners would be heading back toward the finish in less than twenty minutes. It felt like forever.

Finally, a few girls and their unreadable bibs appeared between two pine trees. Cheers began erupting from the bystanders lined up along the course. The red and white colors on the third-placed girl—that was Joan.

As she neared, she picked up her speed. She passed the second-placed girl with dexterity and held that position, pulling away from the now third-placed girl and striding toward the first-placed competitor.

"It's too soon," said Coach. "She'll burn out once she hits that second lap on the track."

Clara scrutinized Joan's steady, even gait. Her cadence quickened as she passed the first-placed girl and took the lead. "Maybe not. We did run 500 miles this summer, Coach. And she makes it look so easy."

As the leader, Joan widened the gap with each stride through the wide, grassy trail leading toward the track.

Clara knew *when* Joan had started running, but she'd been too afraid to ask Joan about the reason *why* after that first time when she'd queried and Joan had walked away. She feared upsetting her friend again.

After discussing what happened with Mrs. Palentino, Clara had deduced that Joan ran as a coping mechanism. The act itself could represent escape from something. Joan escaped her captor, in a way, by escaping death. With running, she could move farther and farther away from the traumatic event.

What Clara hadn't considered was the fact that running also represented moving toward something. With all of Joan's limitations, she was smart and an exceptional athlete. She ran with what could only be described as passion. In everything else, she struggled to demonstrate her emotions. The way she ran—her fluid, effortless-looking movements—made it impossible for Clara to turn away. She had to know if Joan could keep up the incredible pace.

By the time Joan jumped onto the track, she had separated herself by more than 200 meters. That's when others in the crowd rose to their feet. She and Coach had been standing from the beginning of the race along with a few others in the stands. But now people took special notice of Joan.

The cross country team stood, too, and to Clara's amazement, they cheered.

"Come on, Joan! You can do it!"

"Go, Joan! Go!"

Now that her name had been said, the crowd added their encouragement.

Clara's eyes welled with tears as she witnessed the outpouring of support. "Joan!" she shouted. "Run as fast as you can! Finish strong!"

As if singling out Clara's voice, Joan did as instructed. Her ponytail sailed behind her like a ribbon as she circled the track and began her final lap. The second-placed girl, almost an entire lap behind, would never catch her now. Joan sprinted the last two hundred meters, crossing the finish line at her fastest pace, leaving Clara breathless.

The stadium erupted with applause. Clara rushed down the steps and pushed her way through the crowd. She jumped a bar and landed on the track where the finishers cooled down with wobbly steps.

Except Joan. She stood with her hands on her hips, her eyes downcast. For once, she breathed in and out with deep inhales and exhales. She must've pushed herself as hard as she could.

Clara threw her arms around Joan's damp skin and pulled her into a tight embrace. "You won, Joan! You did it."

Without a word, Joan hugged Clara back. When Clara pulled away, she noticed their parents in the stands. They were hugging each other, too, smiling and cheering. Mrs. Palentino was weeping into her husband's shoulder.

Missy and Paula, both wheezing, approached on unsteady legs. They looked a lot dirtier than Joan from the knees down, almost as if they had fallen on the route.

"Joan," panted Missy. "We just wanted to say—" She bent over her knees, looking ready to vomit.

"We wanted to say you did great out there. Really impressive," said Paula.

"I'm gonna be sick," said Missy.

"Come on." Paula waved at Joan and Clara, her face apologetic as she led Missy away toward the locker rooms.

Nothing would surprise Clara after this. She turned to Joan. "You're the winner. How does it feel?"

Joan raised her gaze. "Good. How do you feel?"

Another first. Joan had never asked Clara a question before. "Like today is the first day of the rest of our lives."

Author's Note

"Today is the first day of the rest of your life."

The inspirational quote that served as a mantra for Clara in the story originated sometime in the early 60's. The actual originator is not known, and the quote is often attributed anonymously. The saying was used as a slogan for Synanon, a 1960's drug rehabilitation organization created by Charles Dederich. Eventually, the group became a cult, and Dederich may or may not have coined the phrase. Other sources suggest the saying originated with an activist/theater group called The Diggers, and others still mention a reference to the quote in Abbie Hoffman's book, *Revolution for the Hell of It*. Generally, sources agree that it was a street saying floating around in the 60's.

Every effort was made to locate the originator of the quote, and to my best knowledge, the most accurate attribution is anonymous.

About the Author

Award-winning author Bria Burton lives in St. Petersburg with her wonderful husband and two wild pets. They will soon welcome their first child into the world. At St. Pete Running Company, she's employed as a blogger and customer service manager. Her love/hate relationship with running is well-documented on her running blog, The Anti-Running Runner (**www.runbriarun.blogspot.com**). She has completed four marathons, over a dozen halfs, and too many 5Ks and 10Ks to count.

The Running Girls is a 2017 Royal Palm Literary Award Finalist. Her manuscript, *Sprinter*, won a First Place RPLA in the Unpublished Women's Fiction category. She's currently submitting the manuscript to agents and publishers. Her novella, Little Angel Helper, is a 2016 RPLA winner. She's also a member of the Alvarium Experiment, a by-invitation-only consortium of outstanding authors. Her short fiction has appeared in twenty anthologies and magazines.

Visit her website to hear her radio interviews, check out her upcoming author appearances, and find more of her writing, including free-to-read short stories:

www.briaburton.com

If you enjoyed *The Running Girls*, she'd love a review on Amazon and Goodreads.

BRIA BURTON

The Running Girls